DARK HUNTER

THE STONE WITCH

First US edition published in 2015 by Lerner Pubishing Group.

Text Copyright © Benjamin Hulme-Cross, 2013
Illustrations Copyright © Nelson Evergreen, 2013
This American Edition of *The Stone Witch*, First Edition, is
published by Lerner Publishing Group, Inc., by arrangement with
Bloomsbury Publishing Plc.

Cover design: Dan Bramall. Cover photo: Shutterstock.

Main body text set in Times LT Std. 17/22
Typeface provided by Adobe Systems.

Darby Creek
A division of Lerner Publishing Group, Inc.
241 First Avenue North
Minneapolis, MN 55401 USA

For reading levels and more information, look up this title at
www.lernerbooks.com.

Library of Congress Cataloging-in-Publication Data

Cataloging-in-Publication Data for *The Stone Witch* is on file at
the Library of Congress.
ISBN: 978-1-4677-5726-3 (lib. bdg.:alk. paper)
ISBN: 978-1-4677-8089-6 (pbk.)
ISBN: 978-1-4677-8661-4 (EB pdf)

Manufactured in the United States of America
1 – SB – 7/15/15

DARK HUNTER

THE STONE WITCH

BENJAMIN HULME-CROSS

ILLUSTRATED BY NELSON EVERGREEN

darbycreek

MINNEAPOLIS

The Dark Hunter

Mr. Daniel Blood is the Dark Hunter.
People call him to fight evil demons,
vampires, and ghosts.

Edgar and Mary help Mr. Blood
with his work.

The three hunters need to be strong and
clever to survive . . .

Contents

Chapter 1

The Curse

The village of Skarsby was in the north, near the mountains. It lay at the bottom of a huge hill.

Edgar, Mary, and Mr. Blood had come to help the village.

"Skarsby is under a curse," said Mr. Blood. "Look. Nothing grows on the land around the village."

They went down the hill and walked along a stream. Nothing grew in the field beside the stream. The next field was worse. There was a huge pile of dead cows in it.

They approached the village. A well-dressed man with a small white beard hurried to meet them. Other people from the village came with him.

"You are Mr. Blood, I hope?" said the man. "I am Dr. Hawkins."

"I came as soon as I got your message," said Mr. Blood. "Please tell me about the curse."

"For many years, this village lived in fear of an old woman," said Dr. Hawkins. "We called her the Stone Witch. She lived in a stone cave, up there."

He pointed at the rocky slope behind them. Some of the villagers looked away. Some even cursed or spat.

"Please show me the cave," said Mr. Blood.

"Very well, sir," said Dr. Hawkins. "Come with me."

He led Mr. Blood, Edgar, and Mary up the slope. The villagers went with them.

Chapter 2

The Witch

As they walked, Dr. Hawkins told them the story.

"The Stone Witch put terrible curses on anyone who did not do as she said. She killed people in very nasty ways. She was very old, much older than anyone else here."

Dr. Hawkins went on, "Then, one day, she came down from her cave and into our village. The Stone Witch called us all out into the street and told us that she was dying. We were not sorry.

"She said that we had to turn her cave into a tomb. We must cover the mouth of the cave with a slab of rock and take food to the tomb once a month."

16

Dr. Hawkins looked grim. "She said that a curse would fall on the whole village if we did not do as she told us. Nothing would grow in our fields. Our cows would die. We would all starve."

"And has this happened now?" asked Mr. Blood.

"Yes, sir," said Dr. Hawkins. "Nothing grows in our fields. The cows are all dead."

"But did you do as she said?" asked Mr. Blood.

"Yes, we did," said Dr. Hawkins. "Her cave is a tomb, and every month we all left her food. We don't know what is going on now. We have done what she told us for seven years."

"Seven years?" said Mr. Blood. "Then we may be in real danger."

Dr. Hawkins stopped walking. A thin slab of stone was leaning against some huge rocks.

"Here is the cave, sir," he said. "It is behind this stone slab."

"I have bad news for you," said Mr. Blood. "Strong witches can cheat death. They put their magic into something else before they die.

"They stay dead for seven years. Then, if their magic is strong enough, they start to take life from other people. The witch comes back to life in a new shape. And she comes back with even more power than before."

The villagers began to panic.

Dr. Hawkins looked pale. "What can we do?" he asked.

"If you do nothing, she will feed on you and grow stronger," said Mr. Blood. "She will soon come back to life in her new shape. Then she will open the cave herself."

"So you have two choices," said Mr. Blood. "You can do nothing and let her come back. Or you can let me open the cave now. Then I will try to stop her."

Some of the people shouted, "Kill her!"

"We do not want her to come back to life," said Dr. Hawkins. "Please try to stop this now."

"Very well," said Mr. Blood. "But I warn you, there will be a curse on the tomb. When I open the cave, the curse will start to act. I don't know what will happen. But I am sure it will be bad.

"Now, I will need some help to shift this stone slab."

Nobody moved.

Chapter 3

Opening

Nobody wanted to help open the tomb.

Mr. Blood sighed. "Someone, please get me a stick."

A very old man stepped forward. He had a long, thick piece of wood in his hand.

"Use this," the old man said, handing the stick to Mr. Blood.

"I will help you," said Dr. Hawkins.

He and Mr. Blood wedged the stick into a gap behind the slab. Then they pulled on the stick.

The slab began to move. It fell away from the pile of rocks and slid down the slope. It made a wild screech as it fell.

Then there was silence.

Mr. Blood walked into the open tomb. Mary stepped forward to follow him. Edgar grabbed her arm.

"Are you crazy?" he hissed. "Didn't you hear the story?"

Mary pushed his hand away. "Don't you want to see what's inside?" she asked. She went into the tomb.

Dr. Hawkins looked at Edgar. They were both worried. Slowly, they followed Mr. Blood and Mary into the cave.

There were lots of strange objects on ledges along the walls of the cave.

Edgar saw small bottles of red liquid and ugly little carvings made out of bone.

They walked on. Edgar was too scared to breathe.

They reached the back of the cave. There was nothing there.

Edgar sighed with relief and put his hand against one of the walls.

Above him, something slipped and crashed to the floor.

Everyone jumped.

Edgar gave a shout of terror and pointed. The thing that had fallen was a human skull.

They all looked up. There were more bones lying on a ledge above them. And there was a rough stone statue of a witch. Words were carved on the rock under the ledge.

Tick tock

Tick tock

Bone to stone

Stone to bone

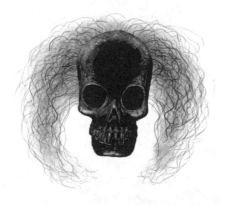

"What does that mean?" asked Dr. Hawkins.

"The witch put her magic in that statue," said Mr. Blood. "We must destroy the statue to stop her."

"But the statue is made of stone!" said Edgar. "How can we destroy it?"

Mr. Blood didn't have time to reply. They heard shouts of fear from outside the cave. They ran out into the light.

The villagers were all standing around the very old man. He was sitting on the ground. A woman began to scream.

Edgar looked closer and gasped with horror. The old man had turned to stone.

Chapter 4

Bone to Stone

"What is going on?" shouted Dr. Hawkins.

Edgar looked over at him. Dr. Hawkins seemed much older.

"What is it?" Mary asked Mr. Blood.

Mr. Blood turned to face Edgar and Mary. His face seemed older too.

"Are you all right?" said Edgar.

There was more screaming. "The witch is coming for us!" howled one woman.

Another old man had turned to stone.

The people began to run back down the slope.

"Time is passing too fast!" said Mary.

Edgar looked over at her. She was standing next to Mr. Blood.

Mr. Blood looked old. He was stooping. But Mary had grown. She was almost as tall as Mr. Blood.

"Quick!" said Mr. Blood. "The witch has put a time curse on us. We are all growing old very fast. And when we get too old, we turn to stone!"

Dr. Hawkins leaned against a rock, panting. He looked very old.

"What do we do, Mr. Blood?" Mary asked.

"Get young people to help," he said. "They will have the most time left. And you must get the stone statue from the tomb.

"The witch will grow stronger every time one of us turns to stone. She is feeding on our lives."

Mr. Blood went on, "There is no time to destroy the statue. So you must find a place to put it where no living person can survive. Then the witch will die as soon as she comes back to life."

"The stream!" Edgar shouted. "Nobody can live underwater!"

"Good!" said Mr. Blood. "Throw the
statue in the stream." Then he turned
to Dr. Hawkins. "Go and call for help!"
he shouted.

But Dr. Hawkins had turned to stone.

Chapter 5

Older

Edgar ran for help.

Mary and Mr. Blood went back into the tomb.

The statue had moved a little way along the ledge. It was moving toward the mouth of the cave.

Mary looked at Mr. Blood and gasped. His hair was white. His skin was pale and wrinkled.

Mr. Blood said, "The witch's statue is starting to move. Her magic is working. You have to get her to the water before she comes to life. After that it will be too . . ."

He stopped talking. His skin went gray.

Mr. Blood had turned to stone.

Mary ran outside and looked down to the village.

Edgar was running back. He was pulling a wheelbarrow with him, but he was alone.

He ran up the slope. All around him, there were people who had turned to stone before they could get home. *How can Edgar run so fast with a heavy wheelbarrow?* Mary thought.

As he got closer, she noticed he had a beard. *He's a man now*, she thought.

"You look different, Mary," said Edgar in a deep voice.

"So do you," said Mary. "Hurry, or it will be too late!"

They rolled the wheelbarrow into the tomb.

"Mr. Blood!" Edgar cried, seeing the statue.

"Come on, Edgar! There's no time to lose!" Mary shouted. "We have to get the witch statue to the stream."

The stone witch was now standing down on the ground.

"The statue is moving by itself!" yelled Mary. "Come on!"

They pushed the stone witch over onto the wheelbarrow and slowly dragged it out of the tomb. There was no track down to the stream. So they slid and pushed and bumped the wheelbarrow down the slope toward the water.

The stone witch's hands and feet began to move on the way.

Down in the village, nobody was screaming anymore. There was no sound at all.

Chapter 6

Stone to Bone

"I can't keep ahold of it much longer," said Edgar. His voice was tired.

Mary looked at him. His hair was gray, his face wrinkled.

She looked down at her arms and saw that her skin looked old too. She gave a small cry and let go of the wheelbarrow.

The statue was too heavy for Edgar to wheel on his own. He let go.

The wheelbarrow began to bounce and tumble down the slope toward the water.

They chased after it. The wheelbarrow stopped at the bottom of the slope, a short distance from the stream.

The stone witch had fallen out of the wheelbarrow. She lay on the ground. Her hands were starting to move, opening and closing.

Mary and Edgar got to the bottom of the slope.

They were weak and frail now. It was hard to walk, but they pushed and rolled the stone witch toward the stream.

Her face began to move. Her legs began to kick.

They got to the edge of the stream.

"Push!" Edgar said.

They pushed the stone witch forward. The statue crashed into the water.

The statue's foot stuck out of the water. It twitched for a few moments, and then it stopped moving.

Edgar and Mary looked at each other. They were no longer an old man and woman. They were young again. They had broken the spell!

"We're alive!" said Mary. "But what about Mr. Blood and the other people?"

The sound of cheering came from the village. They looked back up the slope.

Mr. Blood stood at the mouth of the cave, waving to them and smiling.